SMARTARM

JIM MUSGRAVE

DEDICATION

To the protectors of the nation of Israel.

CONTENTS

FIRST INNING: JAKE AND STOOPY

Jake Golden, age 20, sat down at the end of the bench that was stacked with used shower towels. He was still in his TinCap uniform, and he pushed his cap back on his forehead, exposing his curly black hair. "Can you please pick these up, Stoopy? My allergies are acting up again. I can literally smell the shit stains on these things."

The squat and hunched team clubhouse manager, Brian "Stoopy" Harrelson, moved like a snail to lift the towels, one at a time, and plop them inside the plastic pail. "Listen. I know you got shelled today, Jake. Them towels don't give you allergies. You got an arm that's allergic to balls. Learn to throw straight and them allergies'll go away."

"You don't get extra pay for sarcasm, either, Stoop. You know what a stoop is back in New York, where my family comes from? It's the place where you bounce your rubber balls and visit your neighbors. Who gave you that name, anyway?" Jake took his cell from his pants and began to punch in a number.

"My pa used to call me stupid, but the rest of the family didn't like that, so my mother said I wasn't stupid. I had a back disease, so she said I just looked a little stooped over when I walked. My four brothers took to callin' me Stoopy. But pa always called me stupid."

The diminutive manager pushed the full pail over to his little office next to the showers. Before he shut the door, he said, "Jake, you callin' your girl? What's her name? Susannah? Oh, Susannah! Don't you cry for me!" Stoopy laughed and shut the door.

"Yeah, stupid like a fox," Jake muttered. "Hello? Mister Hirsch? This is Jacob Golden."

Jake! Thanks for returning my call. Listen. I'm going to be in Fort Wayne on business. I want to meet you to talk about your pitching and your Jewish cultural heritage.

"Cultural heritage? Are you sure you have the right guy here? My

1

family's not orthodox. My mother had to fake a heart attack to get us to the table on Passover. We never went to *shul*. My dad said Spinoza was right. God's either everywhere or He's nowhere. We never saw Him anywhere, so guess how religious we were."

I'm not referring to religion, my boy. To be a Jew, you must understand your heritage. To be a baseball playing Jew, you must understand that you also have a heritage to keep in baseball history. Have you heard of the Iron Dome in Israel?

"Yeah. Who hasn't? It shoots down the missiles sent from Gaza and Lebanon before they can hit population areas. What does baseball have to do with that? I thought you might be a baseball scout or something."

No. I'm a computer engineer. I developed the guidance system that goes inside those missile batteries to protect our homeland. An Israeli anti-missile battery works like a baseball team. Take your role, for instance. A pitcher is like the guidance system I created. You have the brains to show the missile battery where to point and how to go where it needs to go to win. I want to make sure your brain is working in the right way, that's all. I know you've been having some problems on the mound, correct? You'll have to teach me about the mechanics of baseball. I'm afraid I'm just an observer, and not a fanatic. However, I do want to see you succeed for the good of the tribe, so to speak.

"Did my dad put you up to this? I don't have money for a personal coach. Did he pay you to call me?" Jake stood up and began to pace around the locker room.

Of course not, Jake. I love baseball, even though I don't really understand the rules very well. However, I've been following your career, and I wanted to give you every advantage these young college studs get. I know you were recruited out of try-outs after high school and that your family has no money, to speak of. I know you can throw the ball 98 miles-per-hour, but you have a problem with control. I just want you to learn about some very specific training I have collected from the research I've done. I have the wisdom of Kenny Holtzman who was called 'The Thinker' by his peers. I also have the pitching strategy of Sandy Koufax, the leftie who actually won fewer games than Holtzman. I know you're a left-hander, and a Jew, so I want to regale you with their teachings in order to put you on the path toward victory. Ultimately, Jake, I want to see you pitch in the majors. So, what do you say? We can meet at the Great Idea. I know it's a bar, but I couldn't pass up that name.

"I don't mean to put you down, Mr. Hirsch, but could you give me a reference or two? I can look you up on LinkedIn, but maybe you have some numbers handy. I'm honestly not trying to get you into trouble. I don't have a great track record as a pitcher, but I can't afford some life coach either."

Most certainly! I'll have my secretary email you my curriculum vitae. It has personal contacts you can call whenever you like. Another thing. I'm not charging you a cent for this help. So, will you be meeting me? Let's make a date. What about next Tuesday after the game with Wisconsin? I have my passport and my glove. What more can a mensch want from life?

Jake put the place, date and time on his smart phone calendar and then punched his girlfriend's number on speed-dial. Susannah Cohen worked as the official blogger for the American Civil Liberties Union in Washington, D.C. Jake met her in high school at DeWitt Clinton in the Bronx in 2009. Whereas she went on to graduate from American University in D.C., Jake pursued his baseball dream. Whereas she was now in law school, he was taking 14-hour bus rides in the Low Class A League.

I saw the score, Jake. Did you try the yoga meditation I taught you? Pitching is all about focus. I thought I was going to fail my Contracts test, but I was able to visualize the elements, and I aced the fucker! Did you even try?

"Look, I never had a picture brain like you do, Suze. I need to do things with my hands to learn them. Listen. There's this guy from Israel, a computer engineer who works on the Iron Dome. He says he wants to teach me how to control my pitches. I'm meeting him next Tuesday at a bar in Fort Wayne. I'm going to text you his references. Could you check them out for me, Miss Good Wife? I don't want to walk into Daniel's lion den without back-up. Howie told me a joke today after I walked three straight guys. You know what the boomer grandpa told his teenaged grandson?"

Howie Brofie should stop playing comedian and start hitting. Catchers are supposed to support their pitchers not distract them.

"I'm going to tell you anyway. The grandpa says, 'When I was your age, we had to walk ten miles in the snow to get stoned and have sex.' I struck out the next two guys to end the inning, I'll have you know. I'll text you the phone numbers when I get them. This guy Hirsch has collected the combined wisdom of Holtzman and Koufax. I hope I don't have to read Proust in French and listen to Broadway musicals in the clubhouse like Kenny and Sandy did."

I'm glad to see you can still laugh after getting rocked 14-3. I'll check this guy's references for you. Are you coming to D.C. during the All-Star break? I want to show you off to my colleagues. Of course, they're big Nationals fans, but they can still talk baseball.

"What's with lawyers and baseball? You'd think they'd be more into basketball and football. I'll be there, but they won't be impressed by my stats."

Baseball's a lot like the law. It's slow, it's deliberate, and you can discuss the rules like they were the Constitution. When they instituted the instant replay challenge, there were orgasmic shouts of joy from barristers across America. It was like that old James Taylor song about the traffic jam. When baseball creates more traffic jams like this so-called 'instant' replay, it's like a legal treatise on Marbury versus Madison. Lawyers love traffic jams! Let's get close-up on this wreck and see why it happened. Just strap me in behind the wheel and bury me with my automobile. My friends will love to take you apart and put you back together, Jake. I miss you, lover. Bye now!

Jake stuffed his smart phone into his warmup jacket pocket as Stoopy Harrelson opened the office door. The sound of the big dryers could be heard as the hunched-over team manager shuffled around to each of the club house doors and locked them up for the night.

"Hey, Stoop! You want to scarf a burrito with me over at Mamacita's? I want to tell you about this guy from Israel. He thinks he can teach me to throw with more control. You know, like Norm Sherry taught Sandy Koufax? Just one Jew helping another Jew."

Stoopy smiled. "Yeah, all he told him was not to grunt so much. Throw the fastball slower and you can control it better. Duh! Did you call Susannah? Are you going to see her?"

"Certainly, my dear stoopmeister! We're going to have an all-star game of our own in Washington," said Jake, draping his pitching arm around the short man's bent shoulders.

Stoopy looked up into the warm brown eyes of the young pitcher and grinned. "You wearing your uniform into town?"

"Yeah, so what?"

"After your pitching today, I'd keep that jacket on. If anybody sees 'Golden' on your back they might mistake it for a target and pitch a burrito at it."

"I don't think so. There were—what--twelve people at the game? We're in last place, Stoop. I want to change all that."

SECOND INNING: AFTER HIRSCH

After his meeting with Saul Hirsch on Tuesday, Jake called Susannah from inside the clubhouse. Stoopy kept smiling over at him as he swept and mopped the floor in front of the lockers. The TinCaps lost their game with Wisconsin, 4-2, and Jake had spent his time in the dugout thinking over what he had learned at their meeting. He was so excited about his revelation that he needed to share it with someone.

His parents believed his baseball sojourn was an aberration. They kept encouraging Susannah to tell Jake how useless it was to believe he could make it to the major leagues and to help him get a job as a legal clerk or (God forbid) enroll in law school.

Susannah had just completed her Agency class, so her mind was a bit frazzled, but she was happy to hear from Jake. *What's going on, lover? How did your Jewish confab with missile man go? Does he want you to be a double-agent? Does Israel want to get a team into the majors? What's his hidden agenda, J?*

"You're such a skeptic, Suze. You checked out his character references. You tell me what his motives are." Jake switched his smart phone to Bluetooth and stuck the bud in his ear.

He's kosher, that's for sure. He won the Presidential Medal of Freedom and Netanyahu has him on his advisory committee. I just think these kinds of people always have something they want to accomplish that's more important than the individual. What did he tell you? Maybe we can read between the lines.

"It was totally awesome. Really. So, he doesn't really know much about how baseball is played. You know, the rules of the game and how they affect strategy? But what he does know from his research is mind-blowing. After we met in the bar for a drink, I spent eighteen hours up in his hotel room, wired to hundreds of electrodes pasted all over my body, and what I learned from this data input has made me a changed human. That's right. I am no longer the Jake Golden you knew before. I have been completely reconfigured for success on the playing field. In fact, my brain was so fried after all those hours of brainwashing that I slept in his room until noon the next day. I almost missed today's game with Wisconsin."

Eighteen hours of brainwashing! Oy gevalt! Are you sure you're still a mensch? Maybe you're a mud man—a golem. This guy probably wants to control you like the Manchurian Candidate.

"No! It's not that kind of brainwashing, Suze. Saul has given me an entirely new way to look at my role as pitcher and how I should understand the game of baseball. He told me exactly what I was getting programmed into my brain, and why he was doing it, and you must never tell this to anyone. In fact, I want to wait until we can see each other in person before I give you the details. This kind of stuff can cause a team to hack into another team's database to acquire the information. Just the way the Cardinals were recently accused of hacking into the Astros' computer system. Saul says this is the new high tech world of baseball, and we must learn to apply the latest technology to win. He chose me to be the prototype for an entirely new era in Jewish player development."

Jewish player development? I told you. He wants to start a new team. You're just the first piece in his Israeli secret plan. They probably want to start a new professional league in Israel like the one that folded after one season in 2007.

"Wrong again, Sherlock Cohen. He told me about that. That was a fiasco and pipe dream of American Jews in Israel. Hirsch says he wants to completely change the American pastime from the inside. His method is to use computers and the programming of the human brain to create a new paradigm of play throughout the system."

Jake, how many times have I told you that today's modern nationalist Israel no longer plays by the rules of international fair play. Remember all the neo-conservative Jews who persuaded our congress under the Bush family? Talk about programming for war! Wolfowitz was getting his marching orders from Netanyahu, and the United States was soon creating that quagmire in the Middle East that exists until today. Remember the Axis of Evil? Right out of the Neocon's playbook. High unemployment in the Muslim countries was what really caused these terrorist groups to thrive and recruit their players. Every smart person knows that. And this guy Hirsch is on Netanyahu's personal advisory committee? Oh my God, Jake. What have you gotten yourself into now?

"Slow down, Susannah. Why do you always have to politicize everything? This is baseball, not international politics. Saul Hirsch wants to help me pitch better. Me. Jake Golden. That's it. I'll tell you all about it during the all-star break. I do miss seeing you. We can't mention any of this to your lawyer friends, however. Hirsch did say that what I was learning could change baseball forever but in a good way. I trust him. I really do. He's like a father I never had. He believes in my talent, and he wants me to succeed."

And what am I? Chopped liver? Your family wants you to succeed also. I just don't want you to think there's some miracle method to catapult you into the major leagues. Whatever this guy Hirsch's telling you, I don't believe he has the key to replace hard work and dedication. Sorry, Jake. I'm a bit old-fashioned in that way.

"Wait until you hear all the details. I promise you, Suze. The method he has is completely innovative, and I have never looked at baseball like this before. I love you, and I love that you're sticking by me through all of this."

Be well, lover. I'll see you in D.C. next week. Maybe you can go out with me to the demonstration.

"Demonstration? What is it this time? Save the dolphins? Stop the gluten epidemic? An acid reflux memorial out by Abe Lincoln?"

Stop it, Jake. You know I belong to the Jewish Voice for Peace. We're demonstrating on the Capitol Mall against the Netanyahu government's policy of confiscating Arab land and turning it over to those machinegun-toting settlers. Don't get me started.

"I think I'll pass on the demo, Counselor. I've never been the politico like you. I'm the jock, the cheese deliveryman, the 98 mile-an-hour whiz kid. You'll be surprised by what I've learned about pitching in only eighteen hours. I can promise you that."

After the call, Jake began to pace the locker room. His mind was focused on some of the information given to him by Hirsch's programming. When he passed by the ball bags, Jake reached down and picked one of the balls up and began to fondle it with both of his hands.

The circle. It's the counter-point to the geometry of the baseball diamond. Just as the star is the nucleus of the planetary system, so is the baseball the center of all that revolves around it. You, Jake, are the controller of this nucleus, this star in the systematic chaos of geometry around you. Feel this ball for the first time. I know you've felt it before, as a child, as a young boy dreaming of his heroics on the mound. Why a mound of dirt? It's to poise you above the fray, is it not? Sixty feet, six inches away from home. You control the power over that home plate, that disk of Euclid's dreams, where everything converges in the heat of the moment. The moment of scoring runs by your opposition. The moment of arcing your ball toward that pendulum of doom, the bat, the vehicle of terror that can swat a ball over one hundred miles per hour back at you—blind you like Herb Score was almost blinded by Gil McDougal's line drive. Score was a lefty power pitcher like you who lived in a dark room as a broadcaster and never really came out of that darkness. Now, I am giving you the chance to be the light that shines through all the line drives, the shattered bat shrapnel rocketing toward you, the runners stealing home, the hitters digging in like tanks on the battlefield, leaning over the plate, your home plate, your place of peace and quiet until they attempt to shatter that round sphere you hurl toward them to defuse your power over the sport. I am returning you that power, Jake. Smell the ball. Turn it around in your hands. Those seams are the woven links, like

Indra's Net, holding together your private universe of circular concentration. You can mold your fingers into the ball like a man holds hands with infinity. Feel its power? The possibilities of rotation are almost unlimited. We have programmed them. The spin on the ball, whether it's scuffed or moistened, what happens when the ball is without spin, the knuckle effect, we will explore the vast reaches of baseball physics. You will need to know this in order to guide the players behind you. You are the spin-doctor, like the modern journalists, you control the way the game is seen by the fans and played by the players. We will give you the power of spin, the power over home, the power over the game itself. Get ready, Jacob Golden, to get rocketed into a new dimension of glory for you and for your team.

Jake sat down on the bench in front of his locker. The baseball in his hand was pressed firmly against his forehead. He was attempting to push the ball through his frontal cortex, the seat of all decision-making in the brain.

Stoopy saw this and was so concerned he had to snatch the ball from Jake's palm, and it took him two attempts to do so. When the baseball was finally extracted, Jake's palm slapped against his forehead so loudly that he looked like Curly in a *Three Stooges* comedy. The tears coursing down Jake's handsome face, however, were not at all humorous.

THIRD INNING: THE ALL-STAR BREAK

When Jake met Susannah and her lawyer friends at the restaurant on K Street in D.C., he was anxious to get her alone to tell her about what he had learned from Saul Hirsch about pitching. In his game against Bowling Green, Jake's pitching arm had taken on a new life of its own. The rotation on his two-seam fastball was such that it plunged like a sinker. His arm slot was working like the bead inside a sharpshooter's scope, and his windup was the "wave of energy" that Koufax taught to power pitchers like Jake. Jake had emailed the animated .gif to Susannah to show her what this meant:

Sandy said that the more you made your entire body into a pitching machine that pushed maximum thrust and every ounce of weight behind the throw, the more you preserved the wear and tear on your muscles. Ken Holtzman said basically the same thing, but he also believed in keeping a book on every hitter. You needed to know the location that got the specific batter out and also what kind of pitch drove him to distraction. Using the title from Marcel Proust's most famous novel, he called the pitcher's book *Remembrance of Things Past.*

Jake began his book that day against Bowling Green. Hirsch had given him a login to the most up-to-the-second database of baseball statistics ever created. All Jake did was type in names of the line-up he would be facing, and this data minutia filled into his tablet screen inside the clubhouse before the game. Only Stoopy saw what he was doing, as he was the last one out of the locker rooms.

"Hey, professor, what're ya doin' there? Research? Did Oh Susannah get you into law school?" Stoppy was dragging two bags of bats behind him when he stopped to lean over Jake's shoulder.

"Did you know some people can remember by sensory association? I could never memorize the way most people do. Susannah, for example, has a photographic memory. She instantly pulls up a picture of what she's studied in her mind's eye. Saul Hirsch showed me that I can remember by associating a certain touch, sound, smell or taste to what I need to recall." Jake pointed down to the leadoff hitter in the Bowling Green lineup. "See this guy, Pettigrew? He can't hit anything thrown low and inside. I remember this by associating him with mushrooms. Every time he comes to bat, I will smell the soft loamy round caps at his feet. I then just try to pound the dirt around his feet to smash those fungi with my pitches. So, you know, 'Pettigrew mushrooms around his feet' is a sentence that comes to mind whenever he comes up to bat. I've done this with every batter, Stoop. I know what they can't hit, and I apply my sensory remembrance to keep it stored in my pitcher's random access memory. Pretty cool, huh?"

The four lawyers Jake met in the restaurant that day worked for the American Civil Liberties Union. Two of them, Chad Worthy and Rebecca Karman, handled civil law suits, and the other two, Sid Bloom and Dave O'Shaughnessy, worked the criminal courts to defend their clients. They all loved the way Susannah wrote about their cases in the blog, as she had a unique way of injecting levity into some pretty boring trials.

Jake spent the luncheon answering questions ranging from why he thought he could play professional baseball (he could throw over 95 miles per hour) to who he believed was the best Jewish baseball player of all time (Hank Greenberg). They were good-natured legal stiffs, as lawyers go, and they weren't focused on themselves the way most lawyers Jake had met seemed to be.

They all wore cargo shorts and tees at this Mexican restaurant. One of them wore a Washington Nationals cap, and he was the first to address Jake.

"Have they ever compared you to Koufax?" Sid Bloom asked, packing his tortilla high with grilled onions and peppers from the fajita platter.

"I think every Jewish pitcher who's a leftie and can throw over 90 miles-an-hour gets compared to Sandy," said Jake. "But, I'm a pretty social guy, whereas Koufax valued his privacy. Also, I like Hippie music from the Sixties and early Seventies, whereas Sandy likes show tunes. The only thing we have in common is the fact that we both had control problems early in our careers."

"Hey, right! Show tunes in the clubhouse." said O'Shaughnessy. "I heard Koufax quit teaching the young Dodger pitchers at Vero Beach when he heard they were calling him gay behind his back. Could it have been those strains of 'I Feel Pretty' from *West Side Story* streaming throughout the clubhouse?"

"I think it's kind of tragic that he pitched before the era of Tommy John surgery," said Rebecca. "We're big L. A. Dodger fans. As Fairfax Jews, we know every Jew who ever played for the Dodgers. Koufax and the Sherry brothers signed photos in my father's den. Imagine what Sandy Koufax could have accomplished given a second chance!"

"Speaking of control, Jacob won his game yesterday against Bowling Green. He struck out fifteen batters and walked none," said Susannah, tilting her head back and dropping a long strand of green pepper down into her mouth. Her curly black hair was frizzed into a Jewfro, her eyes flashed at Jake, and her eyebrows rose, as she swallowed.

The conversation continued about baseball, and about Jews in baseball, and when Jake and Susannah finally exited the restaurant, the lawyers had all promised to text Jake often, and they even offered their legal counsel if he needed it in the future. Chad Worthy said he had negotiated for some professional athletes in his side practice, and he would love to do Jake's deal with the Padres. Jake thanked them all and had collected all their cell numbers.

Back in their hotel room, Susannah told Jake to wait in the bedroom for her to "change into something more comfortable." She also did her best Lauren Becall imitation. They both liked to binge-watch Noir and other movies from the 1940s, and Humphrey Bogart and his wife Lauren Becall were two of their favorites. She sat on Jake's lap, pressed her lips against his, and when he was good and hot, she stood up quickly and swayed over to the bathroom, standing there in the actress's pose, in her sports bra and thongs, before the mirror on the door. "If you want me, Jake, all you have to do is whistle. You do know how to whistle don't you?" she asked, puckering up her full red lips. "You just put your lips together and blow."

The romance was broken, however, when she came out of the bathroom, and Jake was naked, waiting under the covers. Although she was also naked, Susannah was wearing what appeared to be a big red apple over her head. And, on top of her head there was the "tin cap," in the form of a big tin cooking pot. The TinCap's mascot, Johnny, was the persona of one Johnny Appleseed, and Susannah had recreated his likeness very well, except for the curvy torso below the cap and apple head. She was certainly quite an improvement over the emblem Jake wore on his cap and sleeve, which was this:

Jake did, indeed, pucker up his lips and whistle. "C'mere, Johnny," he said. "You're the apple of my eye, so let me polish you until you're really red. I want to plant my seeds in your fertile soil."

Susannah laughed, tossed first her tin cap and then her apple head into the air, and ran over to him, squealing with pleasure as she leaped onto the bed. The minutes of first passion demonstrated two bodies that knew each other very well and were getting reacquainted. As the moments turned into more caring experiments, the breathing and heartbeat of the young lovers encapsulated and enthralled their bodies and finally took over the conscious thoughts of both participants until they were completely devoured by passion.

Later, as the sun outside was deserting all the lobbying and tourist cavorting going on in the nation's capital, Jake and Susannah were devouring some room service Crème Brulee. Susannah licked the browned topping of the dessert from her spoon and smiled over at Jake, who had already finished his portion in three humungous bites. They were seated in opposite chairs with the standing serving tray between them.

"If you made love the way you eat, we would not be compatible, sir," she said, in her best lawyer's voice.

"So, I wanted to tell you what I learned from Saul Hirsch. I guess you were right about his having an agenda. In fact, he says he wants to provide the same high tech counseling to other Jews in baseball," Jake said.

"Oh? So, he doesn't expect to make much of a profit then. Don't you find it rather suspicious that he wants to help only Jews?" Susannah swiveled the tray around to the side, and placed her hands on top of Jake's two large pitcher's hands. "I wasn't too pleased to hear about this guy being an advisor to Bibi 'want-to-bomb-you' Netanyahu. It makes me suspicious that he has some nationalist reason for doing all of this."

"What's wrong with Jews wanting to help other Jews? Netanyahu was re-elected because he keeps his people safe. Saul Hirsch is part of that safety net, and his interest in Jews in baseball is just a cultural interest and not a political one," said Jake, a furrow beginning to crease on his forehead.

Susannah knew she was getting them into one of their least favorite arguments, but she kept pursuing it anyway. "Oh, and now they live in sweetness and peace huddled inside their armed fortress of walls, drone aircraft and now an Iron Dome home protector. Meanwhile, Bibi and his party sneak those orthodox settlers into Gaza and other Arab lands, which pisses Hamas off, and the peace accords go into the toilet. Then he invades Gaza and lobs tank shells into U.N. schools. Thanks for asking about my demonstration at the Capitol Mall, by the way. It went quite well."

"Let me ask you something. What if, instead of relatively peaceful Mexicans and Canadians living on your borders, you had people who didn't recognize your right to exist as a nation? Also, since they were pals to some very rich oil sheiks and other such characters, they could smuggle in missiles and other creative weapons of war to launch at you from time to time? In addition, instead of working peacefully inside your country, these creative immigrants began to blow themselves up inside your universities, your city buses, your restaurants, your night clubs and just about every other high traffic spot in your country. How soon do you think the United States Government would begin to build walls and checkpoints to keep these kinds of terrorists out of the country? What about it, Counselor? Do you see my point?" Jake's face was beet red after this tirade, and he was breathing rapidly, as if he had just faced the league's best hitter.

Susannah, much more poised and collected, pulled both of Jake's hands up to her lips and kissed them. "You keep revising that same tired argument, lover. This is Netanyahu's old song and dance. It was also used by the Bush Administration over here. Basically, it's a false analogy. Israel has treated the Muslim population like crap since 1948. If they had given them a path to citizenship instead of building a sectarian government, Israel might have been able to integrate Muslims into society more easily, and these extremist groups might not have risen up to fight with extreme methods. It's all about economics, Jake, you know that. The income gap. It's much more pronounced in a nation that has its legal system run by the orthodox, and its best jobs kept strictly for the 'chosen people.' We want Israel to create a real constitutional democracy and not a theocratic dictatorship as it has been since its inception. This will prevent the government from using fear tactics in order to repress and slaughter Muslims and continuing to reject Palestinian statehood."

Jake stood up and began to pace the way he did before a big game. He was tired of arguing with Susannah. Besides, this wasn't what he was going to discuss with her. He wanted to talk about baseball and his new career. He was finally on the fast-track to the big leagues, and she was distracting him with the same tired argument that came between them.

"Saul Hirsch provides me with special technology that hooks me up to instant baseball statistics. He has also collected the wisdom of two of the greatest pitchers—Jew or not Jew—in the history of the game. He has given me a way to remember things the way you can remember them. I associate batters with my senses the way you can picture your stupid legal formulas to pass tests. Do you think I was able to pitch that way against Bowling Green because he gave me a yoga meditation mantra? No, Saul says this technology will be sold to others when the time comes. He just wants to keep it private, so to speak, until we can work the bugs out. I was chosen because pitchers have a bigger stage than other positions. In fact, he taught me a whole philosophy behind the pitcher's role on the team, but I don't suppose you'd like to know that."

Susannah stood up and walked over to Jake. She wrapped her arms around his waist from behind and hugged him. "Slow down, champ. You know I'm with you all the way. Yes, and I do want to know all about this new philosophy of yours. And, if Saul Hirsch does teach his new baseball technology to others, I will be the first to eat my words. However, remember that politicians also say a lot of things to get elected, but once they're behind the wheel, they go in a completely different direction."

Jake turned around and took Susannah into his arms and kissed her. Then, he lifted her, and he carried her over to the bed.

"Say, Suze, can I borrow that apple head and tin cap? I want to bring Stoopy a souvenir from D. C., and this would be a great one. Can we try another round of quiet negotiations? I think we're a lot better together with our mouths shut."

"Of course, my hero! Just remember what philosopher and author Albert Camus said about argument. Once we stop talking then physical violence will soon ensue!"

Susannah was able to twist out of the way just before Jake landed on her, but his wide and muscular left arm was able to capture her naked body in its circular grip, and it slowly, inch by inch, brought her closer to him.

"Ah, but a man's reach should exceed his grasp, or what's a heaven for? By the way, that's Robert Browning. You're not the only literary genius in the room, my dear," said Jake, and he kissed her.

FOURTH INNING: BASEBALL'S WHITE WHALE

Being on the road in the minor leagues is a lot like living the life of a rock-and-roll band. Up to fourteen hours inside a bus requires a certain regimen for ball players that probably doesn't happen to the more liberal music artists. Jake Golden was quickly becoming a rising star on the Fort Wayne Indiana TinCaps, so he was getting a quick lesson on this performance hierarchy of professional baseball.

Since the All-Star Break, Jake had won all of his games, and his earned-run-average had sunk to a microscopic 1.25. As it had been 5.62, the plummeting reduction had been noticed by the higher management. He had even been featured on the Padres' Friar Wire, even though he wasn't yet on the club's radar as a top prospect to watch. There were 30 such players on management's radar, so if one could break into that illustrious group it was a good omen.

Saul Hirsch had told Jake to forget about what management and the press were doing. "They will soon recognize you, Jacob. And when they do, you will begin to need my help more than ever. In order to compete on the major league level, you must understand how this chain of command functions. It's not unlike the military, so you should be thankful you have me on your side."

It was exactly the way the team's manager, Rick Montrose, told them as they boarded the bus for their first long road trip, "If you don't like it, play better." As Jake learned from Rick when he began to pitch much better, this business hierarchy was based on the players and their performance.

During one of those 14-hour road trips, Rick explained to Jake what he had gone through during his playing days. He had made it to the Padres major league team as a pitcher and played three years there before settling in as a manager in the lower Class A Midwest League.

Rick was a short man with glasses, and he always wore a buzz cut, as his father had been a Marine, and Rick was instilled with the discipline of the Corps. He ran his team like a marine drill sergeant, and this was good for the lower levels of professional baseball. Many of the players needed this kind of direction, as they were still getting used to the demanding physical and emotional pressures of the game. He punctuated his conversations with jabs of his finger and the salty language of the military.

"I like you, Jake. You remind me a lot of a kid we had here a couple of years back. We pitchers are like the sharpshooters in the unit. We're all about concentration and style. I called this kid 'the monk' because he never talked to nobody. The little fuck never even socialized on the road. He kept his head in his smart phone, just like you do. He also made friends with Stoopy the way you did. I had to bring him around to meeting everybody by confiscating his phone and getting him to shake hands and talk twenty minutes with everybody on the bus. Damned if he didn't come around, just like you have. He's now pitching for the Pads and is one of the best set-up men in the league." Rick slapped his arm rest for emphasis. "You're moving fast, young man. I'm expecting a call any day now for your promotion to San Antonio. The machine grinds out talent like hamburger, don't it? You're lean and mean sirloin, Jake, and I think you'll carry the load just fine."

"I appreciate your help, Rick. I guess my poor performance was making me shy away from everybody. What would happen if I did get called to the bigs? I know they ride jets and stay in the best hotels. What else is different?" Jake asked.

"I like to use an analogy about the call up. See, this jarhead's son can use some of those educated words, too. A big league team is like a Great White Shark. Do you know how they attract sharks today? No, it's not fish chum or blood in the water. That kind of attraction can get you killed. The best way is to use the Death Metal music method. That's what they use these days to get the sharks away from downed pilots and floating sailors tossed off sunken ships. The sharks think the bass sounds and heavy vibrations are a fish in distress. The Show doesn't call for you. You have to call for it. Imagine you want to attract the giant Orca, the San Diego Padres. They will only come to get you if you play something like 'Hammer Smashed Face' by Cannibal Corpse. That's what you're doing by smashing down these Midwest League lineups. You're sending out the violent tremors that attract the big shark in San Diego. Does that make sense?"

"Yeah, I don't think my law school girlfriend could have put it any better," said Jake. "I suppose I need to extend the analogy a bit more and infer that I'll be a little like Jonah inside Moby Dick. How's that for mixing my metaphors?"

"Ha! Good one, Jake. The major leagues is like being swallowed up by a big white whale! Even though you've got players who try to trick whitey by taking steroids or gambling on games, old Moby survives. The sports writers and owners keep polishing the outsides of that whale until it's pure and bleached like the driven snow, and they just hope they can keep us all trapped inside it long enough to turn a big profit. The only way that can happen, of course, is to keep discovering new food to feed it, and new tricks to teach it, and you know what that makes you, don't you?" Rick smiled.

"Whale food?" Jake asked.

"Damned right! And you better be wholesome and organic, lest you give that whale indigestion. If you don't perform and you don't keep your image spotless, like that whale's outsides, then guess what?" Rick grabbed Jake's forearm.

"I get spit out?" Jake said.

"You end up back with us little fish down here inside the tiny fish bowl, where only the kids pay any attention to you. No more big hotels, big meal stipends, and televised games where they can watch you pitch inside the white whale's belly and be entertained by all the new technology they've crammed inside that orca to make the game more interesting to younger sports fans. The white whale teams go all over the world now to find new kinds of fish to eat, and you're just one of them." Rick leaned back in his bus seat and stared out at the passing Midwestern countryside. "They threw me back after three years, and most never make it out of these little Podunk ponds. Maybe you'll last longer, and maybe you won't. Just remember that every white whale is owned and pursued by a Captain Ahab who's ready to sacrifice every last one of us to get his pot of gold. It really don't matter if you cheat to get there. Most of them only care about whether or not you can perform. The ones who've cheated but couldn't perform are never heard from again. The ones who've cheated but were extraordinary performers are always given some room inside the belly of the beast."

The more Jake talked with Saul Hirsch, the more the prospect of getting into the major leagues seemed possible. In fact, Hirsch had sent him what amounted to pre-formatted lineups of all the players currently on teams in both the Texas and Pacific Coast Leagues. What surprised Jake was the fact that all of the sensory memory images had also been created for him. When he clicked on the name of a player, up popped a picture along with a memory sentence to associate in his mind with what pitch and which location he could get the batter out.

Is this cheating? Jake thought, as he browsed through the hundreds of players. *If it is, then as long as I can outperform the competition, I'll be able to stay inside this white whale. Who knows? Maybe this kind of computerized wizardry will change baseball for the better, just the way Saul claimed it would.*

That afternoon, Jake pitched his fourth consecutive shut-out, defeating the West Michigan Whitecaps, 6-0.

When he got out of the shower, Rick Montrose was standing there with a big grin on his face. "Hey, big fish. Pack your things. You're going to San Anton."

FIFTH INNING: ORTHODOX INVASION

Jaime Campos, the manager of the San Antonio Missions, greeted Jake in person at the airport. As a player on the Padres' fast-track, management had paid for the flight. It was coach fare, but it was certainly a lot more comfortable than the team bus in Fort Wayne.

Jake texted Susannah about his promotion to high-A ball, and she texted him back. *You earned it, lover boy. Good luck with your new team.*

It was a strange experience that day riding out to the stadium in San Antonio, Texas. Campos barely said two words to him, pointing out at the scenery instead. "You can get a decent steak dinner there, and the beer's cheap. Just tell the waiter you're on the Missions."

When they arrived in the clubhouse, it was the same treatment. Nobody came up to greet him or to give him a razzing because he was new. They just nodded to him silently as he walked to his locker. They were playing the first place team, the Midland RockHounds of the Oakland Athletics organization. Jake was pitching, and he thought maybe the guys thought it would jinx him if they reached out to him on game day. They were in last place in the standings, and he was called up to be the boost they needed to get off the mat.

However, as he pulled his uniform on, Jake began to think he was being given the cold shoulder because he was now on the list of the Top 30 Padre Players to Watch. He saw it on his cell phone on the flight there. Jake Golden, Top Prospect #4. He had come out of nowhere to become the fourth best playing prospect on the Padres' radar. He believed this was what gave him the status that kept the other players at bay. In addition, he was a pitcher, and a left-hander at that. Baseball superstitions gave players the intuition of warlocks and soothsayers, and left-handed pitchers were the strangest members of the lot.

Players will wear different socks, thong underwear, pee on their hands, eat the same food, wear the same cap or batting helmet, take batting practice at the exact same time, and kiss the same child, pet, woman or object before a game. Jake thought it was the strangest superstition when he heard that Hall of Fame outfielder and batting champ, Wade Boggs, would always write the Hebrew word "chai" in the dirt with his bat:

"Chai" means "life," and Boggs was as goy as one could get. But because Jake had also seen gang-bangers in New York wearing the golden symbol of the "Chai" around their necks, he didn't think much about it. Jake wore one around his neck because he was a Jew, and that meant he was one of the chosen, so who was the superstitious one?

If Jake were moving into the belly of the great white whale, then perhaps the others were afraid to get too close to him. He was "too hot to handle" in their eyes, and he was to be let alone. Besides, he wasn't going to be with the Missions long enough to save their season, so he was looked upon as a shooting star that would quickly disappear into the stratosphere, leaving behind him a trail of strikeouts and goose eggs on the scoreboard.

Jake walked alone out to the bullpen to warm-up. His arm felt okay, but he wondered how long this magical run would last. Surely he couldn't keep up this perfect string of shut-outs. Granted, the computer was giving him the guidance he needed for each batter he faced, and as he went into his wind-up, the picture would flash and then the sentence would appear. *Up and away, a picture of Dorian Gray*, and the RockHounds shortstop, Hal Gray, went down swinging.

Each batter he faced that night was put to rest, like a zombie being drilled in the head by invisible computer death rays, and the ultimate result was a no hitter thrown by a single pitcher, Jacob Aryeh Golden, the first in Missions' franchise history. The Missions had recently experienced a no-no thrown by three pitchers, but this was something special. Or was it? When the three guys accomplished it, it seemed like a team effort. But this thing that Jake threw was an aberration. It appeared as if a gunslinger had been hired to come into town to take-on the outlaws from the next county, and his teammates were there as bystanders.

After throwing the final pitch, which was harmlessly tapped back to Jake, he turned to throw to a first baseman he had never met. And then, a catcher he did not know came out to the mound to congratulate him. It was as if he were being praised by a bunch of strangers on a train where he had been the engineer who had prevented a train wreck by stopping the engine. There had been no teamwork, no loud cheers, no "attaboy" and "you the man." All of these guys knew their team was going to continue without Jake, so he was simply a ghostly figure who had come to San Antonio to visit and then would be on his way. Oh, and yeah, he did throw that no-hitter on his first assignment.

As he walked toward the clubhouse at the back of Wolff Stadium, he saw a strange sight. Coming toward him from the stands were about ten men dressed in long dark coats, wide black hats with brims, and white shirts. As they reached him, he saw the final clue: the long sideburns or *peyot* of the orthodox Jew.

One of them, a large fellow with a full beard, was holding a metal folding chair, and before Jake could resist, he had unfolded it, and another guy lifted the young pitcher up onto it. They then circled around him and lifted the chair with him on it into the air, singing, "Siman tov u'mazal tov, v'siman tov u'mazal tov, siman tov u'mazal tov v'siman tov u'mazal tov, siman tov u'mazal tov v'siman tov u'mazal tov, y'hey lanu. Y'hey lanu, y'hey lanu, u'l'khol Yis'ra'iel, y'hey lanu, y'hey lanu, u'l'khol Yis'ra'iel, y'hey lanu, y'hey lanu, u'l'khol Yis'ra'iel, y'hey lanu, y'hey lanu, u'l'khol Yis'ra'iel."

The orthodox clan finally set Jake down, but the big guy holding the chair said they would now be following him around to all of his games. "We want to share in your joy as the way is prepared for the *mashiach*." This creeped Jake out, as he remembered his childhood in New York City. He would see these strange characters on the streets in Brooklyn, and his parents told him they were the main reason Jews never assimilated into a culture. "It's one thing to practice one's beliefs inside the privacy of *shul* or inside the home, but these orthodox want their practices to be accepted wherever they go," his father, Ben, told him. "That's where they cross the line," he added.

The players and fans in the stands had watched the emotional display of Judaic revelry with a great deal of interest. A few of them even came up to Jake to shake his hand and pat his back. "Great job, kid! Where'd you say you're from? You bring your private cheering section to games everywhere you go?"

Later, inside the clubhouse, Jake got a call from Susannah. Susannah had no experience with the orthodox, and when she told Jake that they had also appeared in front of the offices at the ACLU in Washington D.C., there was a panic in her voice he had never heard before.

Jake, they stared at me when I came into work! Do you think it's the demonstrations I started against Israel? These orthodox settlers have guns! Should I tell the police?

"Calm down, Suze. This is America. They have a right to demonstrate the same as you, and I highly doubt they're toting weapons. I'm just wondering why these *yiddisher kops* are following me around to my games. They're usually not into sports, and most of them don't make much money, so I wonder who's backing them. I'm going to ask Saul Hirsch if he knows what they're up to," said Jake.

They look so scary! Netanyahu made a deal with them to get re-elected. They're the fastest growing population in Israel because they take the Torah's instruction to 'be fruitful and multiply' literally. Netanyahu's deal with them rescinds that earlier Haredi conscription law, so they can once more sit at home studying Torah, never fulfilling their military service obligation like all the other Israelis must do. While their women work, these guys guard their government-provided homes on Arab land, and take care of the kids with all those guns being waved around like it's the Wild West. I don't trust a single one of them!

The free steak and beer Jake had later at Manny's Restaurant was eaten alone, except for a young sports reporter from the *San Antonio Express-News*. He asked Jake some questions about what he thought was the main reason for his success on the mound. Jake told him he had a strict work-out regimen, but he of course didn't say anything about Saul Hirsch and his computer technology. The little guy with glasses thanked him and left Jake to his meal.

Jake slept that night in a large Victorian house near the stadium where many of the bachelor players on the Missions stayed. His bed creaked loudly, and it took about an hour of games on his smart phone to put him to sleep.

Thousands of orthodox men with automatic weapons shot into the air. The bullets rained harmlessly down on Jake as he stood on the pitcher's mound. The shots fell from the clouds like manna and then quickly turned into loaves of his mother's challah bread for Friday Shabbos. As Jake stood there, attempting to tell the crowd that it was all a trick and that he was a complete fraud, his face began to grow a beard, and his sideburns sprouted into long, curly peyot. From the stands around him, people covered their eyes with their right hands and began to chant in Hebrew, but the words came to him in English, out of the bread as he ate it:

Hear, O Israel, the L-rd is our G-d, the L-rd is One.

Then, they spoke to Jake in a whisper:

Blessed be the name of the glory of His kingdom forever and ever.

You shall love the L-rd your G-d with all your heart, with all your soul, and with all your might. And these words which I command you today shall be upon your heart. You shall teach them thoroughly to your children, and you shall speak of them when you sit in your house and when you walk on the road, when you lie down and when you rise. You shall bind them as a sign upon your hand, and they shall be for a reminder between your eyes. And you shall write them upon the doorposts of your house and upon your gates.

And it will be, if you will diligently obey My commandments which I enjoin upon you this day, to love the L-rd your G-d and to serve Him with all your heart and with all your soul, I will give rain for your land at the proper time, the early rain and the late rain, and you will gather in your grain, your wine and your oil. And I will give grass in your fields for your cattle, and you will eat and be sated. Take care lest your heart be lured away, and you turn astray and worship alien gods and bow down to them. For then the L-rd's wrath will flare up against you, and He will close the heavens so that there will be no rain and the earth will not yield its produce, and you will swiftly perish from the good land which the L-rd gives you. Therefore, place these words of Mine upon your heart and upon your soul, and bind them for a sign on your hand, and they shall be for a reminder between your eyes. You shall teach them to your children, to speak of them when you sit in your house and when you walk on the road, when you lie down and when you rise. And you shall inscribe them on the doorposts of your house and on your gates - so that your days and the days of your children may be prolonged on the land which the L-rd swore to your fathers to give to them for as long as the heavens are above the earth.

The L-rd spoke to Moses, saying: Speak to the children of Israel and tell them to make for themselves fringes on the corners of their garments throughout their generations, and to attach a thread of blue on the fringe of each corner. They shall be to you as tzizit, and you shall look upon them and remember all the commandments of the L-rd and fulfill them, and you will not follow after your heart and after your eyes by which you go astray--so that you may remember and fulfill all My commandments and be holy to your G-d. I am the L-rd your G-d who brought you out of the land of Egypt to be your G-d; I, the L-rd, am your G-d. True.

Thousands upon thousands of people in the stands began to converge toward him like a wave of humanoids. Each person was a robot, and their eyes glittered, and their bodies moved with mechanical precision. They were wearing clothing of the orthodox, however, and when they reached Jacob they suddenly began to converge into one shadowy being. It was the tall form of Saul Hirsch, and his body glowed with the power of the masses. Saul's form fell upon Jacob, and they wrestled in the dirt of the pitcher's mound. The powerful grip of Hirsch's hands was around Jake's neck, and he thought he would soon suffocate, but from within a sudden and other-worldly strength took over Jake's body, and he reversed positions with Saul. Jake's hands were now around the older man's neck, until Saul screamed, 'I give up! Turn me loose!'

Saul's body once again separated into the thousands of orthodox robots, and they all turned toward Jake proclaiming, 'Oh, Jacob, you are now the arch-father. You are now Israel!' They all came at him and began pulling at his arms until Jake could feel his body begin to separate. His tendons stretched, his bones snapped, and the blood began to spurt like a river all over the pitcher's mound.

Jake woke-up screaming on the wood floor of the room. The first thing he wanted to do in the morning was to call Saul Hirsch to find out about the orthodox invasion into his life. Even in a dream, Jake knew he could never have remembered the entire Shema prayer of the dedication of faith. Something or someone had planted it in his mind, and Jake wanted to know why.

SIXTH INNING: THE CHIHUAHUAS

Jake had to call Saul Hirsch as he was flying to his next promotion, the Triple-A El Paso Chihuahuas. Jaime Campos told Jake to pack as Jake was eating breakfast downstairs in the Victorian boarding house. "I guess you impressed some folks with the no-no, kid," Jaime said. "Sid, my clubhouse guy, is outside. He'll drive you to the airport. Good luck, amigo, and maybe we'll see you on the Padres."

The guy who drove Jake out to the airport congratulated him on his promotion and also told him about something strange that happened during the game. "The entire cell phone and Wi-Fi system throughout the stadium wouldn't work. At first, I thought it was just my phone, but then I started checking around, and everybody was down. No signals anywhere, man. This never happened before at the stadium. Funny thing, when those guys with the funny black hats left, the signals came back. Do you know those guys? Are they some kind of hackers or something?"

"I never saw them before that night," Jake told him. "But I'll ask somebody I know about it. Thanks for the information."

Now Jake had two questions for Saul Hirsch. Lucky for him, cell phones and other mobile devices were now permitted on board flights. The number rang in Tel Aviv, and Saul picked it up.

Tzohora'im Tovim.

"Hey, Saul, it's me. Jacob Golden. I'm on my way to El Paso, and I wanted to ask you a couple of questions."

Oh yes, your visitors! I knew you'd be asking. We now have a new program in Tel Aviv. Our friends from the ultra-Orthodox have a very high unemployment rate, but the government has taken my suggestion and instituted a special computer and religious training program at RavTech in Bnei Brak. I have employed some of the best graduates to work with me on your beta program. It's all quite exciting for them.

"Okay, that's pretty cool, but two things happened last night that I can't explain. Number one, when these Heredi were at my game, none of the mobile electronic devices worked. Number two, I had a dream, or rather, I'd call it a nightmare, and in it I could hear the entire Shema. I never learned the Shema, and I can now repeat it back to you word for word. Do these two events have anything to do with you or with your new employees?" Jake shook his cell phone, expecting it to go out at any moment because he'd violated some top security clearance.

Yes and yes. As I told you, this experiment with you is in the beta phase of development. My Heredi technologists were monitoring your performance at the game, and I suppose they had their signals a bit strong. They had to send data back to Tel Aviv, but I'm certain we can work on their devices to fix the signal bug. Thanks for telling us, Jacob! The Shema should be in the memory of every Jew who breathes. I was simply doing you a favor when I programmed you, and I added it to your subconscious memory. You have simply retrieved it in your sleep, and now you can use it for times when things may not be going quite right for you. Consider it a good luck charm, my boy, and use it in good health!

"I won't get into the context of my dream, but let's just say that this prayer wasn't exactly coming from humans. They were more like orthodox androids. Would that make them androdox or orthodroids? And, another thing. My girlfriend, Susannah Cohen, told me there were some of these same Heredi waiting for her at her job. I'll be candid with you, Saul. She doesn't like what the government is doing these days, and she belongs to the Voice for Peace in Israel. Were these guys there to harass her in any way? If she loses her job or is harmed in any way, I am out of here. Got that?" Jake's face was getting red as he spoke, and he tried to contain himself, but he found himself saying the first words of the Shema in his mind in Hebrew. *Sh'ma Yis'ra'eil Adonai Eloheinu Adonai echad.*

Calm down, Jacob. There is no relationship between these two events. The only Heredi I have employed are the ones who came to monitor your pitching progress. The ones at Shoshanna's job were there of their free accord. So, now that you are moving quickly up the performance ladder, we must begin a new phase of development. The competition at the major league level is much more difficult. Batters can make adjustments to pitches much quicker, and the teams have their own computer equipment to analyze data. Are you ready to receive an upgrade? I must warn you, we are entering into entirely new technological territory, but the result will ultimately show the world how the sport of baseball, and possibly other sports, can become much more advanced and exciting to watch and to participate in.

"What will the upgrade do? Do you need me to go somewhere to do it?" The plane hit a pocket of turbulence and Jake tightened his grip on the armrest. Flying wasn't his favorite means of transportation.

We'll get things set-up at the Holiday Inn at the airport in El Paso. We've intercepted some internal communications by the front office of the Padres, and we think you'll be getting promoted shortly. That means we have to act quickly to have you ready for your big test against major league batters. Meet us at the hotel on next Wednesday at six in the morning. We'll text you the room number when it's finally ready, all right, Jacob? Also, from here on, you cannot tell anybody about what we're doing, is that clear? That includes immediate family and your girlfriend.

"I understand, Saul. The upgrade must be top secret. I'll be there on Wednesday. I hope you're right about the Padres. This is getting really exciting for me, as you might expect. I owe you a lot." The pilot came on the flight intercom and announced they would be landing in El Paso in ten minutes. "We're landing now, so I have to go," Jake said.

Shalom, Yaakov. Be well, my son.

Jake was able to get introduced to all the players and staff of the El Paso team. At this level, it was common knowledge that Triple-A was the waiting room for the major leagues. It was also understood that when a player was introduced, it meant he was on the fast-track.

The television and other media sport coverage were there, and Jake, for the first time in his life, felt important. The years he spent growing up and dreaming of this day made his heart swell with pride. The years of being the guy with the rocket arm and no control were over. When the female reporter from the San Diego television station came up to him after the introductions, he was ready to respond.

"Jake Golden, you've had a meteoric rise in a short span of three months. What do you hope to accomplish if you make it to the Padres?" she asked, and Jake looked directly into the red light of the camera and not at her.

"I want to show fans that a starting pitcher can be the center of attention again. We've gotten off-track with the modern application of specialists like set-up men and even left-handed guys who come in for one batter. Did you know Cy Young had 749 career complete games? That's the guy they named the pitching award after. Yet, today's starters are lucky if they pitch four complete games in an entire season. I'm going to show America that a starting pitcher can be the superhero on the diamond."

"Wow, that's quite a bold statement," she said. "Aren't you afraid that the players' union will get upset? That will get rid of quite a few jobs."

"All I know is that we're paid to perform. With a smart arm, the starting pitcher should be the rock of Gibraltar upon which a team is built. Gibson, Koufax, and Roberts all completed over twenty games each season. I aim to be the first starter to finish over thirty, and I hope to begin a trend. I also want to show how the starter can be the leader on the field."

"The leader? Don't you think the catcher is better suited for that? Doesn't the pitcher need to concentrate on getting the ball over? Leaders must know what's going on all over the field, don't they?" She flicked her blond hair back and bit her lower lip.

"I'll be showing what I mean by doing it. That's all I can say." Jake turned and walked away from the reporters, but he could hear them arguing amongst themselves. The words he had spoken had not come from the old Jacob Aryeh Golden, he knew that. They were coming from the deep recesses of his being, and he couldn't help but believe they contained a hint of prophesy. A Jewish prophet? Go figure.

The story of Jake Golden was on the major sports news wires that day. One of the kinder headlines said, "Rookie pitcher wants to establish complete game record." But, there was another one which read, "The entitled generation comes to baseball. Rookie wants to be the star of the show."

When Jake took a cab out to the El Paso Airport on Wednesday, he was still feeling mentally drained by all the attention he was getting by the media and by the management of the Padres organization. The media, which stood behind the players, was attacking Jake's rather independent stance with vehemence. They pointed out that it had taken years to develop the union and the representation protections built into the system, and now this one rookie was challenging it all.

On the other hand, the top management of the Padres had met him privately, and General Manager, J. T. Palmary, who made it known to Jake right away that he represented the board of owners, said the Padres welcomed such candid opinions from a fine player of his obvious talent, but he told Jake he should "tone it down" until contract negotiations were a reality.

"We believe what you've expressed does, in fact, represent the best interests of the team as a business, and we will support you when the time comes. As long as you can perform on the field, we will be behind you," said Palmary, his tanned and handsome face beaming over at Jake from across the desk. "Let's just make it our secret for the time being," he added, and Jake had agreed.

The big Heredi who had carried Jake in the chair after he threw the no-hitter greeted him inside the hotel room. The room was number 18, or "chai," and Jake had smiled when it was texted to him.

"*Shalom, Yaakov*! Everything is prepared. Please be seated."

Another one of the orthodox men was seated at a swivel desk. Upon the desk were two syringes, alcohol, gauze, and what looked like a liquid drug of some kind in a small bottle.

"Give me your arm. We must put you under for the upgrade, and it is a painless procedure, I promise you," he said. His crisp white dress shirt almost glowed under the ceiling light, but Jake felt nervous putting his physical wellbeing under the control of these men.

"Where's Saul Hirsch? I want to talk to him first," Jake said.

From the back room came the tall computer engineer and scientist. He had darkly Semitic good looks. His curly black hair was greying at the temples, but his wide forehead and piercing brown eyes gave him the intellectual look that his clear bass voice commanded. He hugged Jake and kissed him on both cheeks in the European fashion.

"Today will mark a turning point in your life, Jacob, and I am eager to establish your leadership role in our community. Benjamin must inject you because you will be unconscious for several hours. When you awaken, I promise you, a new world will open to you. I also want you to know that soon after you have been upgraded, we will be opening up our technology to other players on the Padres, but you shall remain their leader at all times. This will become clear to you once you have been upgraded. In effect, the entire San Diego Padres team will be performing with the most advanced method of sports enhancements science can provide. You will be able to understand what I mean after we upgrade your system. Are you ready, my boy?" The older man led Jake by his left arm, his pitching arm, over to the chair next to the Heredi with the drug.

Jake extended his left arm out to the man, and he felt the firm grip of his fingers as they pulled his muscular arm toward the square of gauze in his right hand. The moist contact of the alcohol hit his skin, and Jake shivered involuntarily. The Heredi filled the syringe carefully with the mouth of the small bottle pointing down toward the needle. He pulled down on the plastic plunger, and the liquid filled the syringe's compartment with clear drug. He then stuck the needle's point directly into the vein inside the crook of Jake's arm, gently pushed in the plunger, and instructed him, "Count backward from ten, please."

Jake began counting, "Ten, nine, eight, seven, six . . ." and his eyelids drooped, and his mind could think of nothing but sleep. He was very tired, and darkness greeted him within seconds. Just before he passed out, Jake could hear the beginning of the Shema being prayed in Hebrew.

Sh'ma Yis'ra'eil Adonai . . .

Jake Golden pitched only one game for the El Paso Chihuahuas. He completed all nine innings, threw a two-hit shut-out, and struck out fifteen batters. No ball ever reached the outfield, and Saul Hirsch had negotiated Jake's contract secretly with the Padres management. At that same meeting, an agreement was also made to allow every player on the 40-man Padre roster to get a chip implant that they would receive on the road after being secretly drugged in a hotel. The Heredi went from room to room with the surgeon, performing the minor surgical implant, which would allow the communications to take place from their new leader and team captain, rookie pitcher Jake Golden.

SEVENTH INNING: THE GOLDEN GOOSE

There have been nine players to hit sixty or more homeruns in a season. From 1927-1998, a span of seventy-one years, only Babe Ruth and former New York Yankees outfielder, Roger Maris, had hit more than sixty homeruns. From 1998-2001, San Francisco Giants outfielder Barry Bonds, St. Louis Cardinals first baseman Mark McGwire and Chicago Cubs right fielder Sammy Sosa, hit sixty homeruns a combined seven times. These three players have also been linked to steroids.

In 1981, the Baseball Players Association called a strike to respond to the owners demanding compensation for losing free agent players to other teams. There were 713 major league games not played that year. Many analysts believe that there was a cause and effect relationship between the use of steroids in the 1990s with the baseball strike of 1981. Attendance was down after the strike, and the initiation of a homerun competition was just what the baseball business needed to increase interest and fan attendance at the games.

Now it was 2018, and there were strict regulations in place to screen for the use of performance-enhancing drugs. However, when Jake Golden was called up to the San Diego Padres in early September of that year, the team was in third place in the Western Division, and they were hoping to reach the playoffs. The last time they were in the playoffs was in 2006, and they again lost to the St. Louis Cardinals, three games to one.

The Padres were playing those same Cardinals when Jake walked out to the mound to pitch for the first time in Petco Park, San Diego. The Padres had been on a seven-game road trip. The contract between J. T. Palmary and Jake Golden had been negotiated, and the owners were aware of what it entailed. The agent for Jake was Saul Hirsch, and Saul had made the 20-year-old left-hander a millionaire two-hundred times over, with a five-year contract. It was what existed between the lines of that contract that mattered most when Jake pitched that day.

Standing on the mound, Jake pulled at the front of his jersey. The blue Padres lettering felt embossed and swollen like it was tattooed into his skin. As he threw his eight warm-up pitches, he glanced at the first Cardinal's hitter. In his mind, the image and sentence flashed of a red wagon and the words "Gabriel Rojas's red wagon outside in the rain." Jake knew to throw fastballs outside to get him to swing.

His catcher, Jerry Farber, threw down to second base, and the ball was tossed around the infield and finally arrived back in Jake's glove.

Jake felt a vibration in his head as he glanced around at the defense behind him. Rows of images were displayed in his field of vision, each image that of a position player on the Padres. With each pitch he selected based on the statistics that were coming to his mind over the network, the players were updated as to where that specific Cardinal's batter most likely would hit the ball. The signals were sent to the players, and then they moved to the designated spot in order to be properly aligned according to the statistical data.

Why do I need to know their names? Jake thought, going into his Sandy Koufax "energy wave" wind-up. *I am the transmitter of data, not a true leader. Why did I ever agree to this? The element of chance has been reduced so that the game is rigged. I only wanted to get an advantage based on knowledge, not on artificial intelligence.*

The machine-like 20-year-old became a vision of computerized efficiency. As each hitter in the Cardinal's line-up came to bat, it looked as if he were participating in a baseball video game that had been hacked into to favor one side over the other. A few hits were "allowed" to drop, but the ultimate result was a 6 to 0 score at the end of the game. Jake Golden had pitched another shut-out, this time at the major league level. However, working inside his mind was a feeling of discontent that could not be accessed by chip implants and the power of suggestion.

As each player high-fived the others at the pitcher's mound after the game, Jake was still there, having pitched a complete game. He had 10 strike-outs, no walks, and every player behind him had been given a chip implant while asleep on the road to receive defensive instructions by WiFi.

Dick Enberg, the Padres television announcer, even had a nickname for Jake: The Golden Goose. The name harkened back to a popular closer for the Padres, Goose Gossage, but Enberg explained his nickname for Jake over the airwaves.

"In the fairytale, everybody who touches the feathers of pure gold on the goose stuck together. What I saw on the field today was a demonstration of a team playing together as if they were stuck to the golden arm of Jake Golden. Let's hope this Golden Goose can lead our Padres into the playoffs this season!"

The announcement came from the Rob Manfred, Commissioner of Major League Baseball that all the teams were now using WiFi communications to align the defensive positions on the field. The only team using chip implants in the "web" between the player's thumb and forefinger was the San Diego Padres.

In addition, it was not known by Major League Baseball that one particular player, a rookie pitcher on the Padres, was also serving as a virtual router to direct all activities on the defense. This was the hidden portion of the contract that team management on the Padres were going to keep top secret until they decided it was time to offer the technology, for a price, to the league as a whole.

Unlike his previous life before the upgrade by Saul Hirsch, Jake became a walking digital application. Everywhere he went, his mind continued to project the vibration of the artificial intelligence that had been implanted inside his brain. His motions became mechanical as well, as he discovered he could communicate with the technology around him.

At a crosswalk, he could change the signal instantly to "walk." He could wave his hand to open electric doors, connect automatically to every remote observation camera and cell phone, and tune into any television, radio or mobile device in his immediate area of vision.

The sensory stimulation was, at first, exhilarating. However, as his brain reached overload, he became depressed, longing for the quiet moments of his life as a child, sitting in the grass watching clouds, or daydreaming out of a window. There was no dream world in this new electronic age of hyper-vigilance. He was suddenly plugged into the grid of electronic reality over which most of the industrialized world was solely dependent. It fascinated yet frightened him to the core of his being. It was as if his very soul were now a part of the computerized controllers of the world.

The remotely controlled car bombs blow up, shattering glass, tearing apart human limbs, torsos and heads. Drones fly over the target, whirring, the geometric pattern fixing upon a house, a building, an automobile, and Jake could hear the mechanical buzz of the Peacekeepers moving into action. The voices of the remote 'pilots' in control thousands of miles from the target repeated their instructions inside Jake's head. The banks, the companies, the homes of private citizens, are open for Jake to inspect and survey. Nothing is private to this new intelligence he now owns, and the power of it keeps Jake's body shaking like a leaf until he can turn it off with alcohol.

The only way Jake could turn off the noise and visions was to drink. He discovered this one day as he sipped a beer watching the replay of his performance on the field, and the artificial intelligence became less of a bother to him. He would drink three or four beers, and his mind returned to an almost normal state of reflective observation. The strange connections disappeared, and his thought patterns became waves of easy energy. He knew that pitcher Dwight Gooden of the Mets once pitched a complete game under the influence of LSD. The brain was a powerful computer, capable of overcoming all kinds of interference and distractions.

However, Jake often became despondent and angry, and he would get into bar fights on the road. He forgot to call or text Susannah, and she would get on him about it. *WTF, J? txt me dork!*

He was a complete loner again, as the players on his team became connected to his electronic control world and were no longer individuals. The players were the HD graphics inside his head during a game, and even when he met them in person, on the flights to other cities, and inside the hotels, he would simply buzz a signal of greeting remotely into their chips, and they would return the greeting. They could also exchange favorite plays they made or some other video recording of the game, but nothing was shared of a personal nature. Maybe some stock tips, but that was about it.

As the season progressed, all Jake did was work-out, pitch, eat, and control his teammates on the field. The only respite was his hours of sitting in front of the television or some other digital screen and drinking himself into a state of tense yet quiet stupor. He would get up from his seat, infrequently, looking for a way to release the pent-up fear inside him, looking for an escape route that could release him from his private hell, but he never found one.

EIGHTH INNING: THE LAST UPGRADE

Jacob Aryeh Golden received the last upgrade to his system just before the final playoff game with the Cardinals. He was set to pitch the contest, and a victory for the Padres would mean a trip to the World Series, the first appearance there since 1998. Before he got the remote upgrade, however, he spoke with Saul Hirsch. Jake wanted to know why he was feeling so depressed and also why his life had taken on such a macabre reality. Was he being controlled by the powerful WiFi system? Why had it taken so much of his focus? What created the digital distractions that ran through his brain at all hours of the day and night?

"Hello, Saul, this is Jake Golden."

Jacob! We've done it, my boy! Your team is on the verge of going to the World Series, and I don't doubt you'll perform just as well in that competition. It will put you on the world stage, and we can then proceed to market our technology to change the sports world forever.

"But my life is pure hell! You never told me about all the abilities I would have outside the game. Why am I able to connect with other digital programs and devices? How do I get information from drones and other high security operations? What if my government finds out I can spy on them? Won't I be arrested? And I have to drink myself stupid to get some quiet inside my head. What the hell, Saul? What's going on here?"

Did you try the Shema? Remember when I told you it would come in handy? What we program into you is all necessary.

"No, I guess I didn't try that. I told you my family was never very Jewish. You're certain it will work?" Jake took a deep breath, and in his mind the prayer was already beginning.

We will be upgrading your system one last time. It will occur in the top of the fourth inning at Petco Park. We have fixed all the bugs you seem to be experiencing, and from that moment on you will be functioning perfectly. We will be officially out of beta. No more interruptions off the playing field. No more feelings of depression. Remember, Jacob, you are also representing the modern State of Israel and all that we represent to the world. We must show the world that we can still produce the technology to make the future both wondrous and secure.

"I'm sorry to sound so selfish, but I just want to be able to return to my life as it was. My girlfriend hasn't seen me in months, and I don't even know my teammates. If this is the future of Israel, then I don't think the world would want any of it." Jake pulled on his jersey with the number 32 on the back. It was Sandy Koufax's number.

Good luck, my boy! Remember the upgrade in the top of the fourth. All will be well after that, I promise you. You will be the most famous Jew in the world after your victories in the World Series, and then you can get betrothed to your bashert, Shoshanna.

"Goodbye, Saul. I'll be in touch. Time to clip the wings of some Redbirds," Jake said, and he tucked his cell phone into the suit jacket inside his locker.

Just before he left to warmup for the game, he heard his cell phone play *I Feel Pretty.* He opened the locker door, took the phone out of his suit jacket, noticed it was Susannah's number, and pressed the phone to his ear. "Suze, what's up? I have to pitch up in here, you know?"

Jake, you have to be careful! Netanyahu has vowed to take action against Iran. He doesn't trust our country's nuclear agreement, and he's vowed to stop Iran's development of nukes. I think this Saul Hirsch is part of this effort, and if he is, then you also might be involved.

"Oh my God. Are you starting that again? Now? Can't you get your head out of politics on the most important day of my career? I told you. My technology is developed for baseball, and any bugs it may have in the system will be cleared up after the top of the fourth inning today. I'm getting an upgrade."

What? You can't pitch today! What if all of this is a front of some kind? Maybe your technology is being used to fight the Iranians. You could be accused as a traitor to your country. Look at Jonathan Pollard. He's still in prison for selling information about American nukes to Israel.

"I have to go now. If you can forget your conspiracy theories for a moment, I would like to see you after the game. We'll be heading to the World Series, you know. It would be great to have you there rooting for me. I think my parents will even be there."

All right, Jacob. You win. But please call me and tell me what happened after your upgrade takes place. I'll bet you're not even supposed to tell me this, am I right?

"Goodbye, Nancy Drew. I'll call you after the game," said Jake, and he stuffed his smart phone back inside his jacket pocket and slammed the locker door.

The score was knotted at three runs apiece when the top of the fourth inning rolled around. There were Cardinals on first and second, as Jake went into his stretch. Jake assumed that the Cardinals had perfected their own WiFi communications system, as they were able to counter many of his defensive moves, and they even got to some of Jake's pitches.

When the upgrade began, Jake was looking over at the runner on second base. He felt a jolt to his nervous system which spread throughout his body and into his left arm. He now felt a speed link in his throwing arm that augmented his eyes to the physical commands being delivered by his brain stem. He had been, in effect, hot-wired to perceive all the qualities of the players, judge their weaknesses, and pass the information into a supremely alert physical balance and very sensitive arm muscle memory. Like a hummingbird, whose perception is so quick that the people in front of him are like statues, Jake had so much time available for decisions that his mind could do anything to make the correct calculation before deciding what to do.

Jake read the calculations sent to him about the runner's current blood pressure, and the figures on how quickly he could get back to the bag after taking his lead. Within a second, Jake had all the information he needed to catch the runner off-guard, and he also knew how fast he needed to throw to the bag to get him out. Jake gave his second baseman the signal by WiFi to break behind the runner and head for the bag. Turning on a dime, Jake threw the ball toward the left corner of the second base bag. The precision of his arm was like a heat-seeking missile, and his throw hit its target within three seconds.

"Yerrrr out!" the second base umpire yelled, and that ended the inning.

NINTH INNING: SMARTARM

The World Series against the Baltimore Orioles was almost an anti-climax. Baltimore did not do any upgrades to their WiFi system, so they could not counter the moves made on the field by Jake and the Padres. In addition, as Jake discovered, his new upgrade gave him the ability to affect play while he was in the dugout.

Jake could focus on a single player in the field and instantly determine his complete physiological status, in real time. He gauged the range of the fielder and where the ball needed to be hit, and he sent this data to the Padres hitter, who processed it, and the chip implant in the Padres hitter's arm adjusted its swing accordingly. The ball was struck at the exact angle and with the precise swing speed needed to bounce the sphere through the gap left in the infield by the fielder's lack of running speed.

In the three games that Jake pitched, he allowed no runs, a grand total of four hits, and he struck out 45. He far surpassed any starting pitcher's performance in the history of the World Series, and, as a result, the San Diego Padres swept the Baltimore Orioles 4 games to 0. The Golden Goose's photo was in every major newspaper and online venue in America.

He could not speak. Somehow, his new upgrade had shut down his oral communication system. When the microphone was thrust in front of him following the final out in game four, Jake tried to speak, but all he could do was open his mouth. The sound he made was a gurgling sputter. The on field interviewer didn't know what to do, so he moved on to the manager of the Padres, who apologized for Jake. "Maybe he's got some laryngitis from all the excitement," said Ross Monahan, the Padres manager.

Susannah Cohen and his parents ran up to Jake. His girlfriend was out of breath, and her eyes were wide. His parents moved to either side of him. His father, Ben, grabbed his left arm and his mother, Sarah, grabbed his right arm. Together, the old couple moved their son out of the circle of media and players, down the steps and into the clubhouse.

Susannah whispered into Jake's ear, "We found some video on Hirsch's server that you must see. I tried to warn you, Jake, but maybe this will prove it to you."

The four Jews entered the Padres conference room and seated Jake at one of the tables. Susannah stuck a thumb drive into the digital projector's USB port and nodded to Ben, who was standing by the door. "Lock the door, Mr. Golden, and then lower the lights," she instructed him.

On the screen, the opening credits ran, and behind it was a mosaic of separate videos showing scenes from the history of baseball being played in the United States. "Hirsch Enterprises Presents the Future Era of Our National Pastime!"

The music was techno, and the voice-over was that of a man with a deeply educated bass, like James Earl Jones or Morgan Freeman Junior.

It was obvious that the stolen video was meant to be seen by owners and not players or fans, as the pitch was made about the technology that could save money and add to the excitement of the game. Jake watched the screen as if it were another WiFi communication inside his system, nothing more, nothing less.

Once upon a time, it was all so simple. Pitchers pitched. Hitters hit. If the stars lined up, somebody with a glove caught what they hit. And that's how baseball games were decided.

Boy, how 1963 was that, huh?

If you think that's how baseball games are decided nowadays, it's very possible you're still listening to music on a 'record player.' And running all over town trying to buy 'film' for your camera. And looking up numbers in a 'phone book.'

Friends, we just don't live on that planet anymore. And neither does the beautiful sport of baseball--no matter how unchanged it may look from afar on your old black-and-white TV 'set.'

Here, instead, is the planet we live on now:

On the screen came the images of Jake and the San Diego Padres. The precision of the defense, the machine-like energy wave of Jake on the mound, and over it all, the voice described the technology behind it.

You already use the WiFi for maneuvering your defensive players on the field. What if I told you that the future of play can mean a competition between teams who can field the best androids?

An animation showed a player with robotic arms and legs and glowing eyes that shot laser beams. The batters clouted mammoth homeruns inside a stadium that resembled an arcade more than a park. However, if the android fielder could get back to the wall in time, he could spring into the air a hundred feet to rob the batter of a homerun. The baserunners ran like greyhounds, their mechanical legs whirring and their slides into bases programmed to maximize all kinds of angles and never damaging the player's limbs the way it was in the old game of baseball.

The cost savings are obvious. Players on the disabled list will be a thing of the past. Your pitching rotation will have three pitchers instead of five, and the real competition will be the team who can process the data faster and move to counter the opposition with a more advanced maneuver.

The scene shifted to a display of all the technology for sale. There was the complete chipset that had been implanted inside Jake. The monitor chips that went inside the other players. The new additions were the artificial titanium arms and legs and laser ocular systems. And then there was the grand control system.

The scene opened on an empty baseball diamond. Something right out of *Field of Dreams.* Into this idyllic setting came the individual android players who all took their respective positions and threw the ball around with laser speed and precise movements. In the outfield, balls came out of radar-controlled guns, zooming toward the fielders, who ran like mechanized gazelles to catch the balls.

And then, the voice-over said: *You will be the master of this innovative epoch in the game of baseball.*

The room filled with the whirring sound of a drone aircraft, and it flew into the picture on the screen above everything.

Each team will have its own control drone, and the battle between opponents will be decided by the people at the highest levels in the game. No longer will you have to rely upon those emotional players and managers who let their simpering passions come between victory and the team. At long last, the behind the scenes management, you, will be getting the full credit for strategies that you so richly deserve!

Susannah shut off the projector, and Ben turned up the lights in the room. Jake was still staring at the screen, and his face had the same expressionless demeanor. It was as if he had been shown something that had already been programmed into his genetic code.

"We've decided that you need to be purged of whatever is in your system, Jacob," said his mother. She reached over and grabbed onto his left hand. He would not look into his mother's eyes, however. He stared straight at the empty screen.

The signal began at the pre-frontal cortex. Jake stood up, and his body reacted to the signal by stepping away from his family and heading for the door. At first, he moved slowly, until the signal became stronger and began to pulsate and vibrate throughout his entire body. When the enhanced buzzing hit the pre-configured pitch, Jake began to run.

Breaking outside into the street, still in full uniform, Jake ran at top speed down Tony Gwynn Boulevard. When the boulevard turned into 7th Street, Jake was receiving his instructions.

Shubach Charter Flight 228 will be at Gate 4, San Diego International Airport.

Jake turned sharply onto J Street, knocking over a homeless man wheeling his shopping cart. Not breaking stride, he ran down J until he reached 5th Avenue. The Sevilla Restaurant and Tapas Bar was filled with customers lined up to go in, and Jake had to push his way through them. Some pointed after him after seeing the name "Golden" on the back of his uniform jersey.

When he reached East Harbor Drive, he did not feel winded at all. The signal was driving him, supplying the adrenaline he needed to keep up his break-neck speed.

Terminal Access Road greeted him up ahead. He ran with renewed vigor into the terminal, past the walking pedestrians rolling their luggage, and when he saw the sign to Gate 4, he turned left and ran down the corridor. A man in a suit was waiting at the gate, and this man turned toward the TSA security guard and nodded. The guard let Jake through without any search of his person.

The top secret flight took six hours. Jake was the only passenger on board, and the only escort with him was the man in the suit. When they landed, the jet's door opened and the man walked Jake down the boarding stairs and onto the tarmac. It was dark, and Jake could hear the noises of the jungle on the perimeter of the small air strip. That's when Jake's vision shut down. He could no longer see or speak. He could only feel the pressure on his arm as he was guided into what sounded like a land rover vehicle.

As he was guided into the concrete bunker building, Jake could again see. His power of speech had also been reinitiated, and he turned to the man in the suit and said, "Where am I? Why am I here?"

"You'll see in a minute," the man said, and he opened a door inside the bunker.

Seated around a circular table were five men, and two of them were in uniforms of the United States Army and Air Force. They were generals.

Jake's escort brought him up to the periphery of the circle.

The Army general was speaking to the group. His eyes had dark circles under them, and his voice was raspy. "Environmental destruction, whether caused by human behavior or cataclysmic mega-disasters such as floods, hurricanes, earthquakes, or tsunamis. Problems of this scope may overwhelm the capacity of local authorities to respond, and may even overtax national militaries, requiring a larger international response."

"I agree, General, but can we afford the inevitable blowback in the communities from this?" One of the civilian men asked. He glanced over at Jake and smiled.

"We all know that an era has begun of persistent conflict due to competition for depleting natural resources and overseas markets fueling future resource wars over water, food and energy. The new antigovernment and radical ideologies potentially threaten government stability," the Army general pointed out.

The Air Force general then spoke. "Hirsch developed this technology to improve the image of Israel in the world. He has his Iron Dome, but now we have this," he said, nodding over at Jake, "we must reverse engineer the device and develop it for our new project."

The man who had escorted Jake cleared his throat. "DoD might be forced by circumstances to put its broad resources at the disposal of civil authorities to contain and reverse violent threats to domestic tranquility. Under the most extreme circumstances, this might include use of military force against hostile groups inside the United States. Further, DoD would be, by necessity, an essential enabling hub for the continuity of political authority in a multi-state or nationwide civil conflict or disturbance."

The group of men all nodded their heads in agreement. The quiet was then like on the day the passenger jets exploded inside the Twin Towers.

"You mean, you would attack your own people?" The words came out of Jake's mouth, but the minute he spoke them he wish he hadn't. The men all turned toward him.

The man in the suit continued, "In 2010, the Pentagon had begun developing a 20,000 strong troop force who would be on-hand to respond to domestic catastrophes and civil unrest. The program was reportedly based on a 2005 Homeland Security strategy which emphasized preparing for multiple, simultaneous mass casualty incidents."

The Army general added, "The following year, a U. S. Army-funded RAND Corp study called for a U. S. force presence specifically to deal with civil unrest. Such fears were further solidified in a detailed 2010 study by the U. S. Joint Forces Command designed to inform joint concept development and experimentation throughout the Department of Defense setting out the military's definitive vision for future trends and potential global threats. Climate change, the study said, would lead to increased risk of tsunamis, typhoons, hurricanes, tornadoes, earthquakes and other natural catastrophes."

Another civilian spoke up for the first time, "Furthermore, if such a catastrophe occurs within the United States itself--particularly when the nation's economy is in a fragile state or where U. S. military bases or key civilian infrastructure are broadly affected--the damage to U. S. security could be considerable."

The last man in the circle said, "A severe energy crunch is inevitable without a massive expansion of production and refining capacity. While it is difficult to predict precisely what economic, political, and strategic effects such a shortfall might produce, it surely would reduce the prospects for growth in both the developing and developed worlds. Such an economic slowdown would exacerbate other unresolved tensions."

The man in the suit standing beside Jake concluded, "That year the DoD's Quadrennial Defense Review seconded such concerns, while recognizing that climate change, energy security, and economic stability are inextricably linked."

"What about me? What are you going to do with me?" Jake was panicked. It was like his worst nightmares were being realized. He could no longer feel separate from the technology inside him. Was there no way out of this horror?

The Army general laughed. "You will become one of the new field officers in our home security force. With your communication abilities, you'll be able to perform in baseball as a cover and then perform as our secret controller to guide our top secret forces against the inevitable rise of civil unrest. We can dispatch drone strikes wherever you find them. We can keep the streets safe, and our homeland will remain secure. There will be no Snowden traitors in our new leadership, Jacob Golden. When the right administration comes to power, you will be the essence of the programmed officer in the new war on terror—right here at home!"

When Jake began to pray the Shema, he leaped at the man in the suit and started to choke him. They both fell to the floor, and it took four of the other men to get Jake off of him.

"Take him to the lab! Get to work at once!" the man in the suit gasped from his prone position on the floor, holding his neck, his face almost turning purple.

Jake was on the operating table when Seal Team Six broke into the room. Along with them were Susannah and Saul Hirsch. The collection of helmeted Navy and Marine Seals arrested the Army and Air Force generals and the other four men from Homeland Security and the Central Intelligence Agency.

Susannah hugged Jake, and tears were streaming down her cheeks.

"How did you find me?" Jake asked.

"Your father put the old-fashioned global positioning chip inside your pocket when he was walking with you inside the Padres clubhouse after the game. Your friend Hirsch said something like this might be attempted. He said Israel has the same kind of right-wing extremists in their government."

"What's all of this mean? What will I become?" Jake was on the verge of tears.

"Jacob, the Shema was placed inside your system for a reason. You were able to break through their hacked program by using it. It will always be there for you to use, even if you decide to become part of our new sports endeavor. It may not seem to be the most ethical or sportsmanlike way to play baseball, but, you must admit, the changes are going to happen," Saul Hirsch said, bending over Jake and touching his forehead. "On the other hand, we can remove all of the technology, if you wish."

"Do you mind if I get married first, and then I can get back to you?" Jake said, squeezing the hand of his *bashert*. "I don't know if I can take too many changes at once," he added, and the three Jews laughed together, enjoying the self-deprecating irony of the moment.

LIFE IN 2050 PREVIEW CHAPTER ONE

The day was again overcast. The marine layer hovered over William as he rode the YST wagon to the heart of the tourist district in Old Town, San Diego. His fellow passengers had their noses in their video screen visors that covered their faces like helmets from the Middle Ages. "Knights in white satin," William whispered to himself from a lyric he was hearing on the audio channels coming from the buds inside his ears. He preferred audio over video because it gave him a background soundtrack for his seditious thoughts. He was also able to see his brothers and sisters with much more clarity. William was turning 40 in three days, and he knew what was in store for him, but unlike all of these other digital monkeys, he didn't trust a single word that came from Big Bro's mouth.

 Inside his Youth Socialist Hostel on Congress Street, it smelled of boiled ramen and yoga mats. At one end of the ranch-style building, at the end of the hallway, a huge hologram vibrated in 16,777,216 bytes of color. It was the gargantuan portrait of a man of about twenty-five, with a blond beard and ruggedly handsome features. William headed for his cubicle domicile four doors down the hall. The rest of the building was dark, as it was part of the "Put Nature First" drive to limit energy use. *Of course, that didn't prevent the infrared spy cameras from being used in every building, in every city around the world*, William thought, limping inside his sparse apartment. His soccer knee was acting up again, and he took some pride at having injured himself playing one of the banned sports. On each wall of every apartment, the same hologram gazed at you, and the eyes followed you as you moved about. The voice from the poster rang out, and it could never be switched-off to save energy or to prevent global weather changes. BIG BRO IS MINDFUL OF YOU, the voice said, in a deep bass vibrato.

Behind his simple cot and clothes dresser, the wall display was broadcasting the party's 24-hour news. It was showing the latest in digital gadgets from the party headquarters in downtown San Diego and how "mindful brothers and sisters were using the entertainment visors and meditation videos of Big Bro to reach new heights of sensory bliss." *Unless you've reached 40. Then, bliss might as well be taking a piss off Big Bro's nose,* William thought, remembering the gigantic statue of their beloved leader out in Balboa Park, next to the old statue of El Cid on horseback. William watched his own reflection in the monitor. He was a thin brother with a curly-black goatee and black racial features. Wide, flat nose with flaring nostrils, full pink lips and pink palms reflected back at him in the mirror image. William's mother, Rose, who had Lewy Body Dementia, thought that mirrors led to another world. Just like *Alice in Wonderland.* "There are no races or categories of discrimination," William smiled and spoke out loud to the spy monitor from Big Bro's propaganda. *We only discriminate against you as you get older,* he thought. "Forty is the new twenty," he spoke at the screen. *Forty puts you on automatic Anomic Suicide watch,* he thought.

Outside, the world looked cold. In the best equatorial spot on the Earth, the temperatures hadn't reached 80 degrees in over ten years. Devil winds were swirling tourist trash into spirals in front of William as he walked toward his place of employment. These were the microcosmic versions of the giant tornadoes, hurricanes and tsunamis that kept the world on guard throughout the year. The oceans had risen to create new waterfront properties on every continent, and William could see the breakers coming into shore from the Pacific about two blocks away. The bearded bro stared down at you from every street corner, and he was the only color in this frigid world of dark shadows. The hologram on the building across the street was looking right at him and broadcasting: BIG BRO IS MINDING YOU, the voice said, as the image's dark eyes looked deep into William's own. Down in the street, another poster, this one of paper, was whipping along in the wind, and William could see the letters YSW across the blue-green image of the world. In the far distance, a drone hovered and then darted, like a dragonfly, between the low hacienda-type tourist traps. They were protecting the Inner Party members, those aged 1-39, who took in the sights and sounds of old San Diego, completely protected by the drones, which could call in an air strike or a "droid doom boom" in seconds, to disperse an unruly mob or individual. The drone patrols didn't matter, however. Only the Mindfulness Droid Protectors, or MDP, mattered.

On another building made to resemble a Spanish restaurant, the same YSW news was being broadcast. The screen could transmit and receive simultaneously, and William knew all the spy devices could pick-up even a whisper from a citizen in the street. A young party member of about sixteen walked toward him, accompanied by two females. They were walking amidst the hundreds of tourists who were taking their children on a walking tour of the pseudo-Mexican structures that looked more like Big Bro's idea of what Hispanic culture was than what it actually had been. The three party members had their telescreen visors over their eyes, and yet the two women were topless and giggling, as the young stud between them masturbated in public to the pornography going on in his private 3D world of illusion. William shook his head in dismay as he passed them.

The world was now broken into pods of control called "Mindful Metro Campuses," and William was serving in the southern quadrant of what used be known as North America. The cities kept their names, and there were vague attempts at cultural identification, as it was in Old Town, but there was no longer any central government other than Big Bro and the Young Socialists World Party. After the War on Terror was declared victorious by the bands of millions of unemployed youth across the globe, in what was believed to be 2028, a new vision for the future was declared, and there was a unique coming together of computer and android technology and the vision of a powerful youth, who decided to snatch the wealth of their more primitive elders and construct a new world order. Religions were banned for the good of the libertarian principles espoused by the new party, and so were any sports, recreation, business or other human endeavor that seemed to promote any kind of collective values or principles other than what Big Bro was declaring as "the only path out of the chaos and militant fear that was our past."

Up ahead stood the tall skyscraper—the only one allowed—of the Young Socialists' Ministry of Mindfulness. This was where William worked, and it was also broadcasting the libertarian message of the party, in ten-foot letters, running every ten seconds across the huge digital banner in front of the building:

WAR IS IN THE PAST
FREEDOM IS ALWAYS TODAY
IGNORANCE IS IN WRITTEN HISTORY

The Ministry of Mindfulness contained four thousand rooms above ground and corresponding fortresses below. Scattered about San Diego, as in every other major metropolitan city in the world, were just three other buildings of the same appearance and size. They were the giants in the land of Lilliputian structures and hostels, and they were the only buildings allowed to be constructed above one story tall. These were the skyscrapers that housed the complete apparatus of government for Big Bro's Young Socialist World Party. The Ministry of Mindfulness, which controlled news, entertainment, meditation, education and the fine arts. The Ministry of Visual Reality, which ran the armies of drones and androids. The Ministry of Freedom, which concerned itself with suppressing any rebellions. And the Ministry of Living Bliss, which maintained economic affairs. Their names in Mindfulvoice: Minimind, Miniview, Minifree and Minibliss.

William knew that the Ministry of Freedom was the most frightening and sinister building. It had no windows, and it was kept in complete darkness inside, as everyone who entered was issued infrared gear and goggles to see. It was guarded 24/7 by android guards armed with laser bio-demobilizing rifles that could cause a human head to explode. You could enter and exit only after having been injected with top-secret computer chips from Big Bro's office inside.

Get the complete serial at our website. emrepublishing.com/join-life-in-2050/

ABOUT THE AUTHOR

 Jim Musgrave was born in Fall River, Massachusetts (home to Lizzie Borden). He worked for Caltech in Pasadena (home of the "Big Bang Theory") and continues to use his fascination with technology in his "Detective Pat O'Malley Steampunk Mystery" series. Jim was also a professor of English for 24 years, and he runs a publishing business with his wife, Ellen, in San Diego. He has won many awards, including being a finalist in the Bram Stoker Awards and the Heekin Foundation Awards. His mystery, *Forevermore*, won First Place in the Clue Historical Mystery Contest in 2014. This is the first novel in the best-selling Steampunk series starring Detective Patrick James O'Malley set in post-Civil War New York City.

www.ingramcontent.com/pod-product-compliance
Lightning Source LLC
Chambersburg PA
CBHW071219130626
46555CB00004B/1767